PLEASE DON'T EAT MY SISTER!

Caroline Pitcher

Illustrated by Bridget MacKeith

See me fight with a posh, flesh-hungry piano!

A & C Black • London

To Max

comix

First paperback edition 2002
First published 2002 in hardback by
A & C Black (Publishers) Ltd
37 Soho Square, London, W1D 3QZ

ISBN 0-7136-5969-6

A CIP catalogue for this book is available from the
British Library.

Printed and bound in Spain by G. Z. Printek, Bilbao

CHAPTER ONE

Lenny crept to the top of the stairs. He could see something crouching at the bottom. It was shivering and it looked up at Lenny with big, white-ringed eyes.

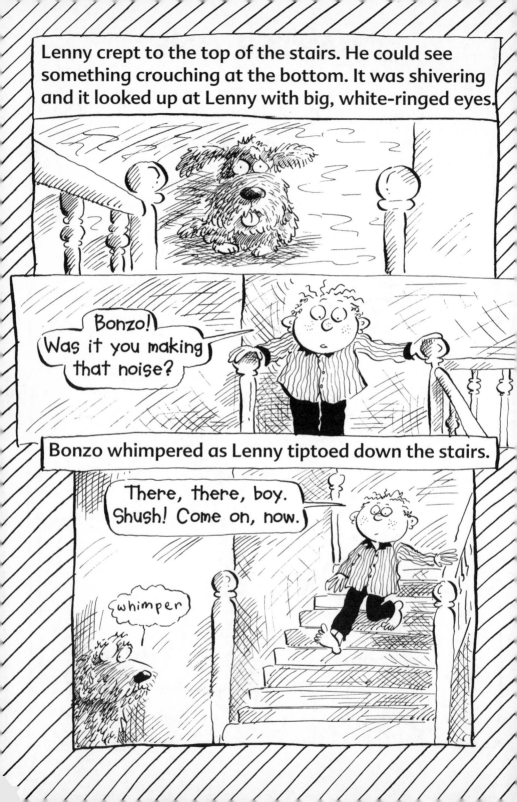

Bonzo! Was it you making that noise?

Bonzo whimpered as Lenny tiptoed down the stairs.

There, there, boy. Shush! Come on, now.

whimper

Lenny picked Bonzo up and carried him upstairs. They snuggled down in bed.

Better not let Mum and Dad know you've been here, Bonzo. You know, for such a tiny dog you've got a very big growl.

But some time towards dawn Lenny heard it again, even louder.

GRRRHOWLGRRR!

It wasn't Bonzo at all.

CHAPTER TWO

As Lenny ate his breakfast he heard someone bashing away at a piano...

♫ p-l-i-n-k-e-t-y p-l-o-n-k ♪

She's good, isn't she? And she's only six! Your sister is a real little Chopin.

Chopin on a bad day... playing Baa Baa Black Sheep?

I don't think so... when did she make a tape, Dad?

It's not a tape. Louise is playing the piano LIVE.

But we haven't got a piano.

We have now. And what a piano!

Dad, that's not fair. If Louise has got a piano, then I should get a drum kit.

8

9

Lenny crept down the stairs. | The noises stopped.

He tiptoed to the sitting-room door and opened it slowly. The room was full of moonlight. The piano squatted in the very middle of the room.

It's like a big black toad, waiting for something.

s-n-a-r-l

The keys gleamed like teeth, white against the dark wood.

You're not alive. You're only a piano. You couldn't have made those noises on your own.

And then the lid flew up and back and the piano snarled, its keys pointed and deadly as tusks...

s-h-i-v-e-r

Lenny ran out of the room and back to bed as if the hounds of hell were after him!

Oh Bonzo, I hope pianos can't climb stairs!

CHAPTER FOUR

Lenny, of course pianos aren't dangerous. We are so lucky to get this one!

Look at the wood, as glossy as a new chestnut. Look inside, under the lid. It's like a beautiful golden harp.

I don't want to look. I might see what it had for supper.

14

16

17

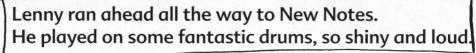

Lenny ran ahead all the way to New Notes.
He played on some fantastic drums, so shiny and loud.

A little figure in a big cape was standing on the doorstep.

Mrs Mazurka! Come in and see my new piano. It's so BIG!

I can't wait to see it, my darling!

Oh! It's amazing. I just must have a play.

Mrs Mazurka threw back her cape, kicked off her boots with their stiletto heels, and raised her podgy hands above the keyboard.

Lenny looked at Mrs Mazurka who seemed to have four eyebrows. She had a spare pair pencilled on that looked like birds flying.

She's so little. How will she ever play this monster piano?

But play that piano she did. And how! The little hammers jumped like golden moths.

From the piano came wonderful music, for kings and magicians, for heroes and villains, for fine horses running and planets whirling.

Lenny felt he was being swept down a river of music, down waterfalls and out to sea.

24

CHAPTER FIVE

That afternoon, the men from New Notes delivered the drum kit.

Here we are, son. You can drive your mum and dad mad with this lot!

Please put the drums in the sitting room next to our brand new grand piano.

Next to the grand piano...

OH NO! Not THAT piano!

You should have seen the old folks' home after it had been there for a week... they were all in plaster.

What do you mean?

We must be going now, sorry!

The men beat a hasty exit. Mum began polishing the piano with a tin of beeswax, while Lenny made a bee-line for the new drum kit.

Lenny was beginning to think he was wrong about the piano. It sat in the sitting room so gleaming and proud and didn't seem angry any more.

HOW WRONG CAN YOU GET?...

Why are you barking, Bonzo? Don't you like my drums? You'll have to get used to them.

Oh... you're barking because someone's at the door.

Lenny could see a shape through the wavy glass, a shape with a huge head...

Oh. It's not a big head, it's big hair. What a very strange man. What very wild hair.

He looks like one of those wire coat-hangers.

35

37

Madam, I am a composer. Perhaps you've heard my concerto for flute and microwave? Or my overture for piano, hair dryer and electric hedge-trimmer?

GULP

No?

Er-no. I can't say I have.

You see, times were hard and I had to sell my beloved piano. It broke my heart. But now, I have recorded my 'Variations for Piccolo and Pasta-maker' and I can afford to buy it back again. The man at New Notes said it has ended up here.

41

CHAPTER SEVEN

That night Lenny didn't get a wink of sleep. The piano wailed and roared and howled a blood-curdling howl. Lenny burrowed under the bedclothes with Bonzo but still he couldn't sleep.

Mum should have let Mr Blatt have his piano back, Bonzo. He's right. It's a genius's piano.

It's not a little child's piano. Unless the child is called Mozart. That piano is miserable here! It'll do something terrible...

Lenny fell asleep just as it was getting light. He slept late and it was twelve o'clock when he had his breakfast.

Lenny dashed into the sitting room. He saw a great big pair of jaws, wide open, like a shark. The piano was trying to eat Louise! Its keys were snapping and gnashing and her legs were sticking out from under its lid.

Hold on, Louise! I've got you.

Lenny forced up the lid of the piano again, one eye on its gleaming keys...

What on earth is the matter?

48

49

But just as they sat down with their baked beans, they heard an unspeakable noise.

ROARWHOOSHCRASHTINKLEBANG

...and then silence... an awful silence...

CHAPTER EIGHT

Fifteen minutes later a big van arrived. Baby piano in...

...angry piano out.

59

But that wasn't the last they heard of Ludwig Blatt.
He invited Louise and Lenny to play in a concert.

They played in 'Fun and Frolics for two pianos, egg whisk and electric drill'. He wrote a special drum part for Lenny, too.

Mr Blatt is like a clockwork penguin. His music is very, very odd. There are plinkety plonks and scrapes and tootles and whirrs just when you don't expect them.

But the audience is going wild! He's so happy he's crying. Tears are flying off him like sparks. And the angry piano? It has been brilliant!

I swear it's giving a great big grin.